leapfrog

Rhyme
Time

# Dan's Gran's
# Goat

First published in 2006 by
Franklin Watts
338 Euston Road
London
NW1 3BH

Franklin Watts Australia
Hachette Children's Books
Level 17/207 Kent Street
Sydney
NSW 2000

Text © Joan Stimson 2006
Illustration © Beccy Blake 2006

A CIP catalogue record for this book is available
from the British Library.

ISBN (10) 0 7496 6596 3 (hbk)
ISBN (13) 978-0-7496-6596-8 (hbk)
ISBN (10) 0 7496 6814 8 (pbk)
ISBN (13) 978-0-7496-6814-3 (pbk)

**Series Editor:** Jackie Hamley
**Series Advisor:** Dr Barrie Wade
**Series Designer:** Peter Scoulding

Printed in China

# Dan's Gran's Goat

by Joan Stimson

Illustrated by Beccy Blake

## W
## FRANKLIN WATTS
LONDON • SYDNEY

# Dan's gran had a goat called Scruff.

His beard was a mess
and his coat was rough.

6

7

"Scruff needs a wash,"
said Gran one day.

"And Dan can help
when he comes to stay."

SOAP

9

Dan came to stay and
he tried not to laugh,

when out of the shed
came an old tin bath.

"Help!" thought Scruff
and off Scruff ran.

So off sped Gran,
and off sped Dan!

Scruff ran to the park.

He slid down the slide.

"Come back Scruff!"
Dan's gran cried.

Dan cried, too.

"It's time to stop!"

But Scruff ran on
and into a shop.

Inside the shop,
Scruff toppled tins.

18

He scattered fruit.

He emptied bins.

He nibbled here,

he gobbled there.

20

He scoffed a pie,

he gulped a pear.

Outside the shop,
Scruff burped and then
he raced on down
the road again.

23

But down the road,
old Mr Rose
had just turned on
his garden hose.

And when Dan yelled:

"Quick! Help us please!"

He gave that hose
a mighty squeeze!

So, in the end,
Scruff got his wash.

"Oh, Scruff," beamed Gran.
"You do look posh!"

31

Leapfrog has been specially designed to fit the requirements of the **National Literacy Strategy**. It offers real books for beginning readers by top authors and illustrators.

There are 55 Leapfrog stories to choose from:

* hardback